A Gift
to the
Young Readers
of Seattle
from the
Paul G. Allen
Charitable
Foundation

P9-DTO-880

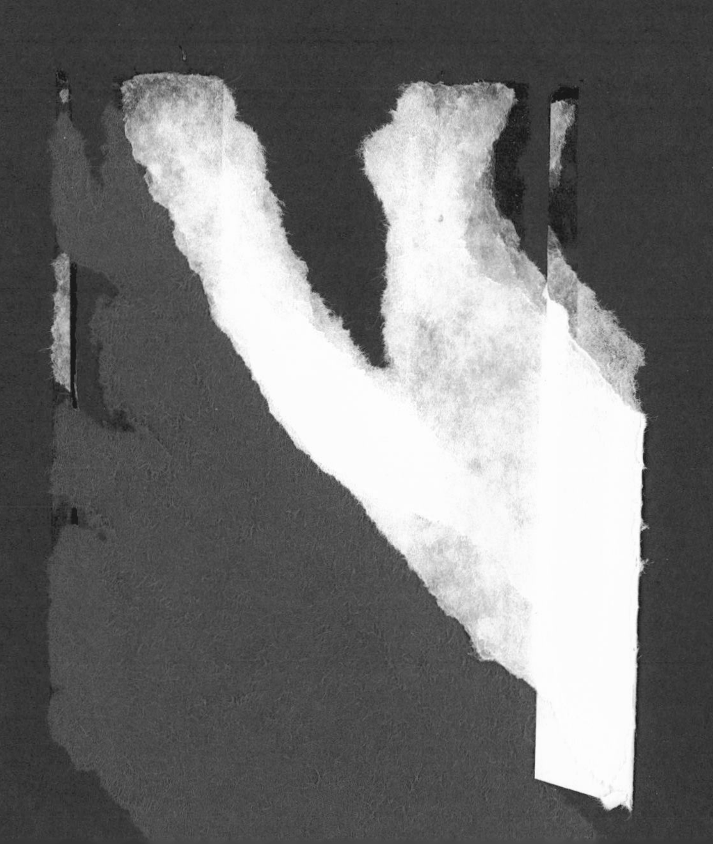

WHAT YOU KNOW FIRST

WHAT YOU KNOW FIRST

by PATRICIA MACLACHLAN

engravings by

BARRY MOSER

JOANNA COTLER BOOKS
AN IMPRINT OF HARPERCOLLINSPUBLISHERS

The images in this book were engraved in Resingrave, a synthetic wood engraving medium manufactured by Richard Woodman in Redwood City, California. They were printed from the blocks by Vance Studley at the Archetype Press, Pasadena, California.

This book was set in Kennerley Bold, a typeface designed by Frederic W. Goudy in 1911.

Library of Congress Cataloging-in-Publication Data

MacLachlan, Patricia. What you know first / by Patricia MacLachlan ; engravings by Barry Moser. p. cm. "Joanna Cotler Books"

Summary: As a family prepares to move away from their farm, the daughter reflects on all the things she loves there so that when her baby brother is older she can tell him what it was like. ISBN 0-06-024413-5. — ISBN 0-06-024414-3 (lib. bdg.) [1. Farm life—Fiction. 2. Country life—Fiction. 3. Moving, Household—Fiction.] I. Moser, Barry, ill. II. Title.

PZ7.M2225Wh 1995 94-38341 [Fic]—dc20 CIP AC

2 3 4 5 6 7 8 9 10 ❖

To Anne MacLachlan—
a kindred spirit.
—PM

For my friend Ann Patchett,
who understands what is left behind.
—BM

I could

If I wanted

Tell Mama and Papa that I won't go.

I won't go, I'll say,

To a new house,

To the new place,

To a land I've never seen.

I could

If I wanted

Tell them to take the baby—

He won't care.

He doesn't know about the slough

Where the pipits feed.

Where the geese sky-talk in the spring.

That baby hasn't even *seen* winter

With snow drifting hard against fences,

And the horses breathing puffs like clouds in the air,

Ice on their noses.

The cold so sharp it cuts you.

I could

If I wanted

Stay here

With the new people,

If they'll have me.

I will live in the attic

With my books

And my paints

And paper so I can write letters

To Mama and Papa

If they miss me.

Or maybe
I'll live in a tree.
The tall cottonwood that was small
when Papa was small,
But grew faster than he did.
Now it has branches
And crooks where I can sit
To look over the rooftop,
Over the windmill,
Over the prairie
So big that I can't see
Where the land begins
Or where it ends.

Or

I'll live at Uncle Bly's house by the river,

Listening to him sing

Cowboy songs

About buffalo

And cattle drives

Lightning storms

And love.

We'll eat pie for breakfast

Because Uncle Bly likes it.

And no one tells him he can't.

When Uncle Bly goes to Cheyenne
I'll live with Mr. Boots, who shoes the horses
And lives in the red barn.
We'll sleep in the hay with our eyes open
Until they drop shut.
Listening
    to the rain on the tin roof
    the wind rattling the windows
Waking when the rooster crows
In sunlight.

My Mama is sad to leave, too.

She cried when we sold the farm—

The baby, in her arms, reached up to touch her tears.

And Papa took a long walk

when they came to take the cows away

after he whispered good-bye to Bess

after she leaned against him

The way she always does.

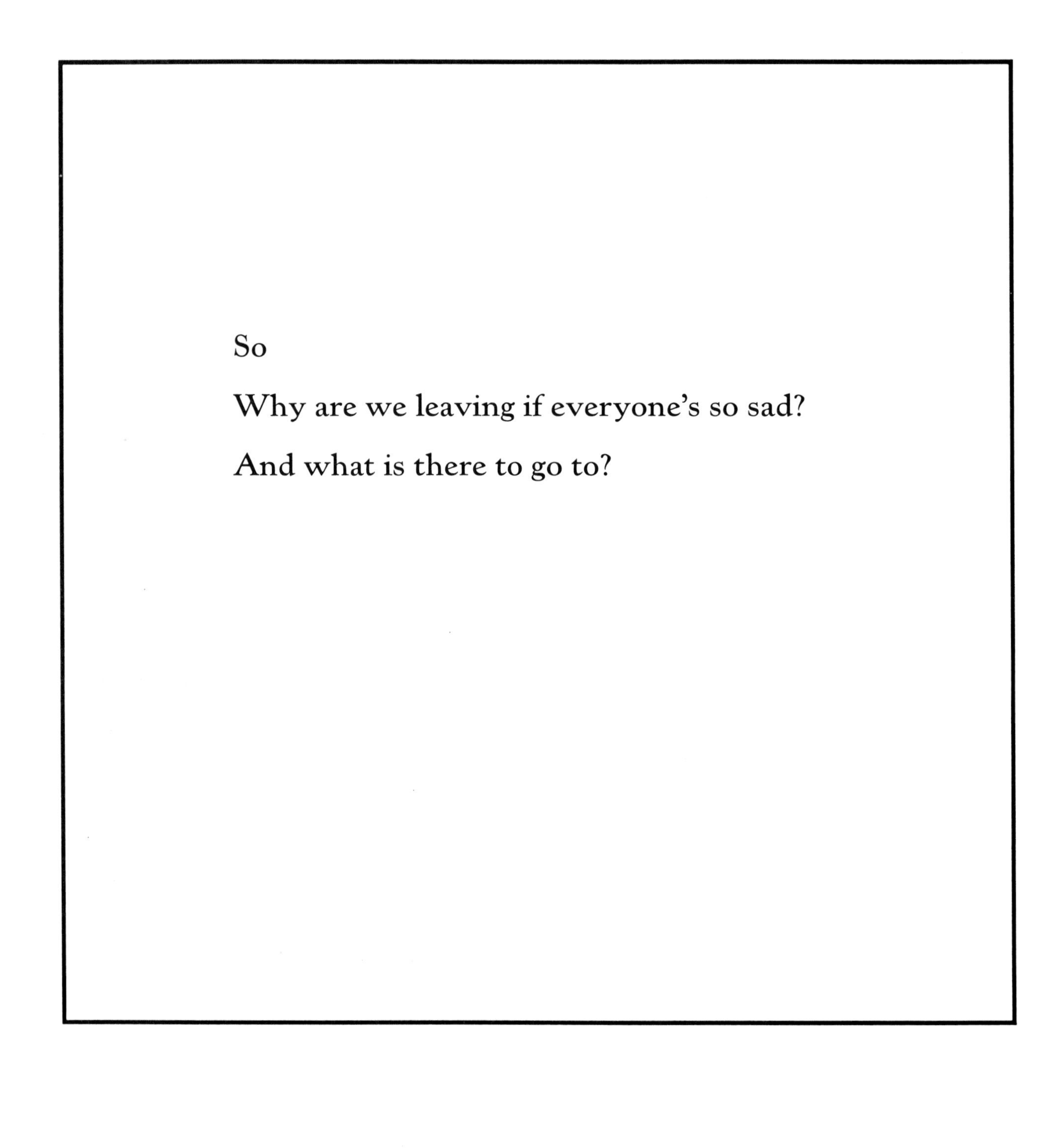
So
Why are we leaving if everyone's so sad?
And what is there to go to?

Mama says there's an ocean

In the new place.

And Papa says there are trees.

I don't need trees,

Only the one.

I don't need an ocean

I've got an ocean of grass.

Mama says the baby would miss me

If I stay.

My Mama says how will he know about the way the

Cottonwood leaves rattle when it's dry,

If I don't tell him.

And how will he ever know Uncle Bly's songs,

If I don't sing them.

What you know first stays with you, my Papa says.

But just in case I forget

I will take a twig of the cottonwood tree

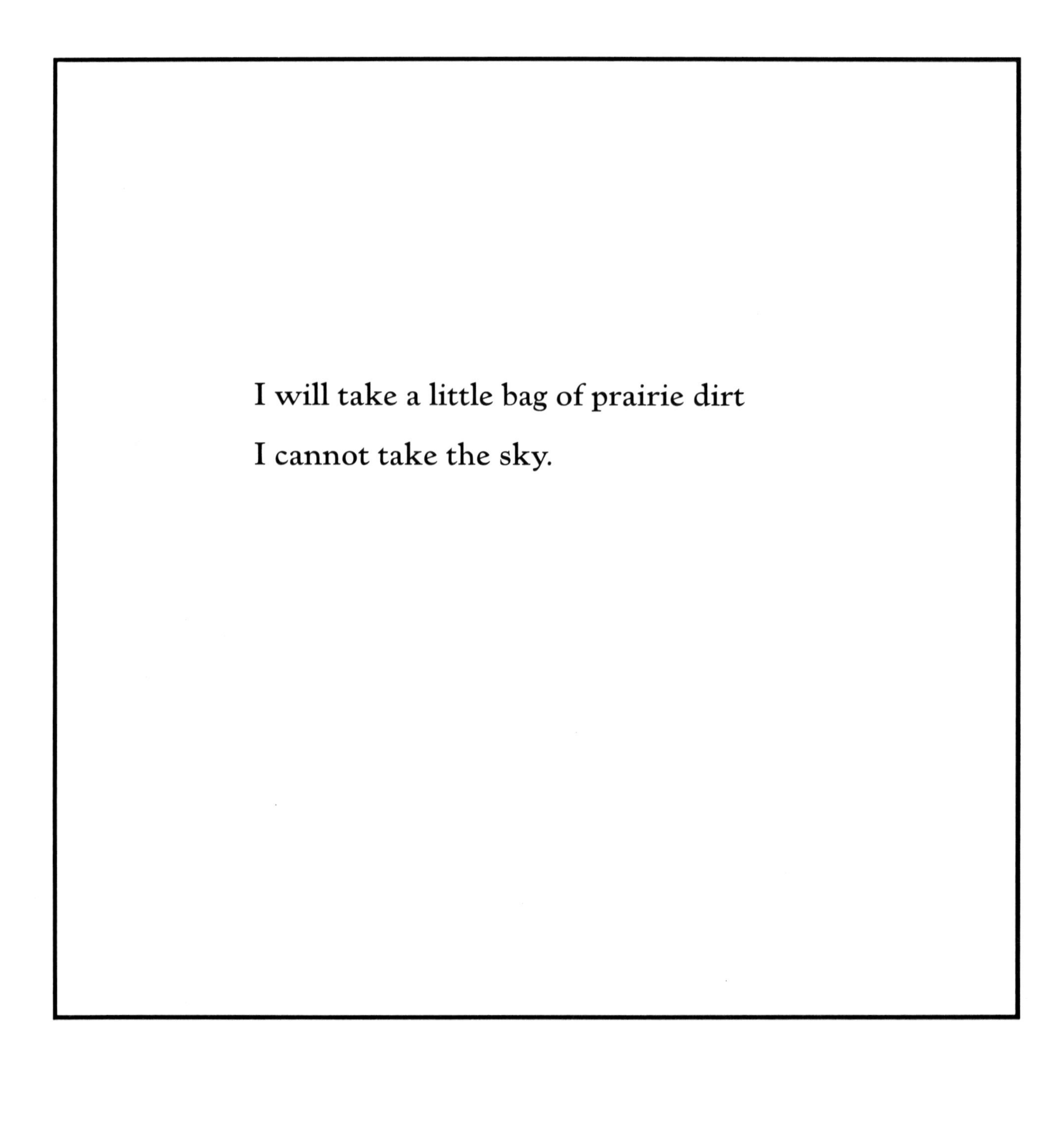

I will take a little bag of prairie dirt

I cannot take the sky.

And I'll try hard to remember the songs,

And the sound of the rooster at dawn,

And how soft the cows' ears are

When you touch them,

So the baby will know

What he knew first.

75-695

And so I can remember, too.